STEPHEN SAVAGE

SUPERTRUCK

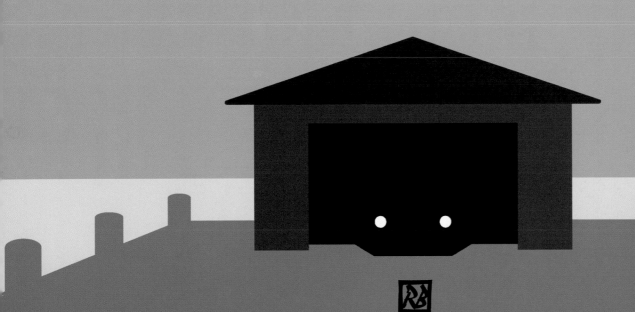

A NEAL PORTER BOOK
ROARING BROOK PRESS
NEW YORK

For my father-in-law, Bill,
who went everywhere in his super truck

Copyright © 2015 by Stephen Savage
A Neal Porter Book
Published by Roaring Brook Press
Roaring Brook Press is a division of Holtzbrinck Publishing Holdings Limited Partnership
175 Fifth Avenue, New York, New York 10010
mackids.com

Library of Congress Cataloging-in-Publication Data

Savage, Stephen, 1965–
    Supertruck / Stephen Savage. — First edition.
        pages cm
    "A Neal Porter Book."
    Summary: "When the city is hit by a colossal snowstorm, only one
superhero can save the day. But who is this mysterious hero, and why does
he disappear once his job is done?"— Provided by publisher.
    ISBN 978-1-59643-821-7 (hardback)
    [1. Refuse collection vehicles—Fiction. 2. Trucks—Fiction. 3. Snow
removal—Fiction. 4. Heroes—Fiction.] I. Title.
    PZ7.S2615Sup 2015
    [E]—dc23
                                                                    2014009901

Roaring Brook Press books may be purchased for business or promotional use. For information
on bulk purchases please contact Macmillan Corporate and Premium Sales Department
at (800) 221-7945 x5442 or by email at specialmarkets@macmillan.com.

First edition 2015
Printed in the United States of America by Phoenix Color, Hagerstown, Maryland

3 5 7 9 10 8 6 4 2

The city
is full of
brave trucks.

The bucket truck fixes a power line.

The fire truck puts out a blaze.

The tow truck rescues a bus.

The garbage truck?
He just collects
the trash.

One evening,
it starts snowing.

It snows and snows and snows.

The city is caught in a terrible blizzard.

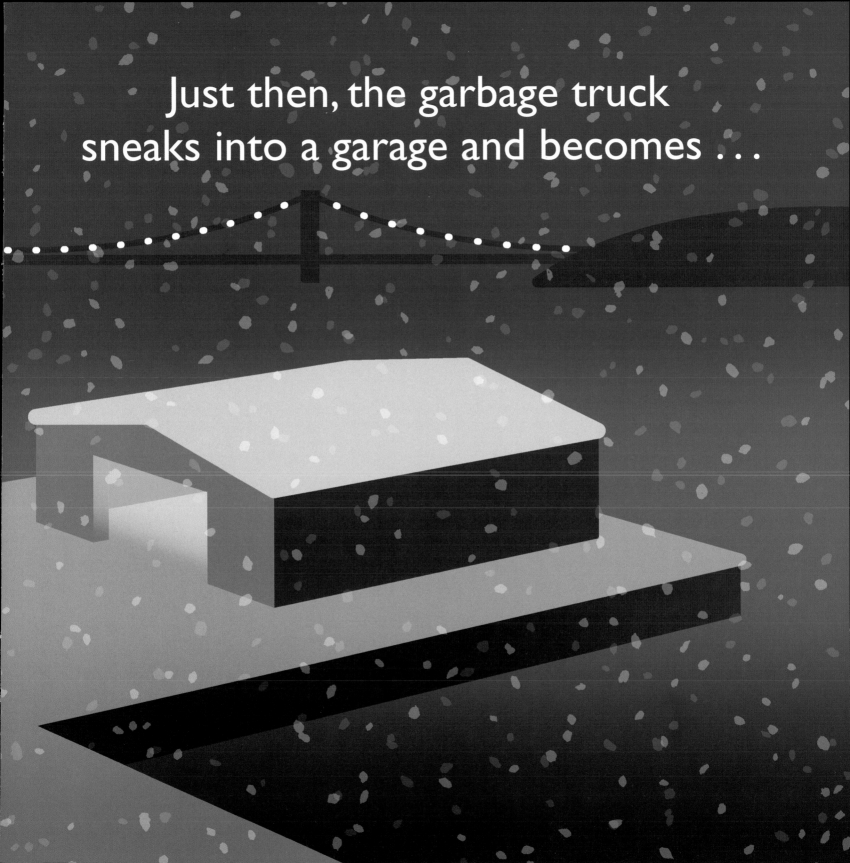

Just then, the garbage truck sneaks into a garage and becomes . . .

SUPERTRUCK!

He digs out the west side.
He digs out the east side.
He digs out the whole city.

Hurray for Supertruck!

The next morning, the trucks
wonder about the mighty
truck who saved them.
Where could he be?

He's just collecting the trash.